Queen of the Hollow

Jacci DeVera

Dark Hollows Press

Thank you to my friends, and my family, Chuck, Rebecca, and Melanie, for not letting me give up. I love you.

QUEEN OF THE HOLLOW

Time and planning, her mother always told her. She had time and planning on her side. Gain the high ground, and then plan some more. On higher ground, Calla had every advantage. She could see clearer and see farther. The *boors* might be stronger, but she was faster. Calla liked the safety of the loft in the house, but Momma preferred the trees. Calla always figured she got her Shifting from Momma. She never saw Momma Change but the way she took to the trees, Calla thought she must have been a Shifter.

Momma would be so disappointed.

In a nervous rush, Calla McAmis had lost her footing and fallen down the icy steps of the front porch. She stared up at the twinkling evening star and blinked back tears. Things were broken. Her leg was bloody. She couldn't move her left arm well. She'd remained in the yard in misery, watching as the sun set behind the ridge, watching twilight deepen. After all her mother went through, and it was to end like this?

She dragged herself to the bottom step, which in no way could be considered high ground. She used her good arm to pull herself up only to have it slip on ice and blood. She cracked her chin on the stair. For an instant, the sharp sting of biting her tongue blocked out the rest. But it was brief. More blood. She might as well send out invitations: Come one, come all, for an easy claim.

The thought made her angry all over again. The anger at herself and her situation had let her reach the stairs. This time, it let her gain the porch. She spit out blood and had to rest. At this rate, she'd be lucky to reach the door before the moon shone over Chicory Ridge.

She imagined the puma shape-shifter *toms*, or *boors*, swarming from every mountain pass and deer trail, descending upon her, taking their claim and eating her alive afterward. It would be her first Change since Momma had died, and the last thing she wanted was any sex-sniffing *toms* showing their whiskered faces.

And not this time of all times—this time was her Heat.

The Heat cycle ran in six months, February and again in August for Calla. The full moon this year fell on the fourteenth of February. It was the Crow Moon, Hunger Moon, the harshest month of the West Virginia year, when everything—animals, shifters, people—had to scavenge for food.

1

The Change occurred every Moon. The Change that came about every six months was harsher, more sudden, without gentleness. It reverberated through her skull like a screeching hawk, complete with piercing talons that ripped at her from throat to waist. Heat, Momma called it. She wasn't sure why. Whether it was February or August, it felt itchy in her skin, cold and hollow and violent, like she needed to be out of it and inside it all at the same time. It made her want to cry, to scream at the moon, but Momma made her be quiet. A raucous would just draw the *boors*.

Outside of a Heat moon, boys would still come. Some. Not a lot. Momma had to kill a couple. Hurt a lot more. Word got around. Fewer and fewer tried—except during Heat. Some forces of nature couldn't be stopped. Protecting her daughter during Heat, Momma was a force of nature, too. Sometimes from the trees, sometimes from the house, but always defending their home.

Then Momma had died. Rake wounds to the leg, the belly, bites on the shoulder. It caught up to her, put her in a fever. They'd gone to town like they did once a month, to get bottle drinks, flour, ammo, alcohol and pharmaceuticals. Especially sulfur drugs which the pharmacy wasn't supposed to carry any more. Calla had started to think maybe Momma knew the pharmacist, or the owner, or both, better than just 'in passing.' Still, they didn't do her any good. Her mother stopped breathing a week later some time before dawn. And Calla had cried, loud, lonely, distraught wailing. The bleak, gray winter days came and went after that. About fifteen maybe since she'd buried her momma near the creek, and she was left in the dark house alone, lost, her heart aching.

Last night she'd lain in her bed, crying, shivering, longing for the Change and praying it wouldn't come. Tonight it would. The moon would make it come. She had thought she'd simply go to the attic loft with the knives and the rifle. She'd be quiet. She'd wait it out. She'd miss her mother and wish she were there to guide her and help her and love her through this. Like she'd always been. If a *tom* crossed the yard from the tree line, she'd shoot him. She just had to wait, and watch, and be patient.

But she'd slipped on ice and now lay like a wounded rat on her porch, unable to get to the safety of the house. She thought something was broken in her leg; something inside too, in her chest. No position relieved the throbbing burn, and she couldn't seem to catch her breath. As she glared at the door just out of her reach, the best she could hope for was that the Change came and the boys, the *boors*, didn't. She would have one night to heal. She would be in better shape to defend herself if they sniffed her out the second night.

Her worst fear was that the Change would come, the boys would come, and they'd tear her apart, devour her until nothing was left. The moon was still below the silhouette of trees. She could feel it. This wasn't how she wanted to die. This wasn't how her mother had taught her. She should've been able to protect herself just as well as her mother had. She'd meet up with Momma again this way. But she'd not made her proud.

Why couldn't the moon just stop? Just once—not climb its way to the top of the skeletal trees of the ridgeline. Just tonight—not get to where it stared down at her hungrily from over the hills. It wouldn't, though. It was a force of nature far older, far more ancient than even Shifter blood.

With something between a sob and a groan, she pulled herself toward the door again. She squeezed closed her eyes and gritted her teeth to keep from crying out and inched to the screen door. If she didn't, she would die out here. If she had to die, by God at least let it be in the house. Not out here where any monster, human or shifter, could just come across and kick her carcass over. She grunted and pushed and pulled and the sobs hitched from her throat, but at last she had dragged herself across the threshold. From the slatted floor, she slammed shut the door and leaned there, panting and trying to stop the sobbing.

She couldn't take a breath that didn't feel as though an awl punching through her lungs. She found herself wishing for unconsciousness. She wanted to close her eyes and go to sleep and forget the pain and the panic. She needed the rifle. She needed the knives. She needed to be in the attic, and any of those things was as impossible at the moment as stopping the moon.

Short of stopping the moon, she couldn't stop the *toms*.

There was a .22 Momma kept by the door. It was just for noise to scare the raccoons away. It wouldn't stop a cat in full Change any more than a BB gun would stop a bear. With a heave she rolled over, clutched the stock of the rifle against her, using it to help brace herself as she lifted her sweaty head to the window ledge and looked out. She couldn't see much—and she could see better than most people, her momma had said. She managed to hold her breath for a couple of seconds but didn't hear anything coming for her.

Maybe. She licked her lips, tasting scabs. Maybe somewhere in all her begging, and cursing, and praying, and crying, God had heard her and the boys would stay away tonight. She'd have that night to heal within a Change, and she could take on a whole passel of *boors* tomorrow night.

Then she heard the low penetrating yowl of a cougar from the ridge. She shivered and bit her lip to hold in a whimper. Had she barred the kitchen door? Were the windows shuttered up and locked? Would it keep out a cat during Heat? She wasn't sure, but she doubted it. Why else would Momma run them off and take harsher measure when they wouldn't take the hint?

The call came again and something inside her rose to answer it; rose in her throat like bile to tell him where she was. But he already knew. They always came to the hollow during a full moon. A body'd think she put out fresh killed chickens once a month, what with the regularity of *toms* visiting. She was panting now, as though hemmed in and needing the freedom to run. "No, no, no, no," she whispered, closing her eyes tight to concentrate, to wish, to pray.

She heard a growl, deep, throaty, close. Her eyes snapped open. It was a different cat. Somehow she knew it instinctively, but it was confirmed when an answering snarl responded from the hillside. She swallowed hard, the ache from holding in sound real and painful in her chest. She tried to take a normal breath but it caught in her mouth and she nearly gagged.

"Please no. Go away," she whispered, only able to lean against the wall between the window and front door, gripping and re-gripping the barrel of the .22. The moon's glow seeped over the top of the ridge and she heard the mournful screeching of a trapped cougar in her skull. She closed her eyes again, drumming her head against the wall of the house, repeating, "No, no, no, no," until the words were garbled and spewed from her mouth like foam. She tossed the gun from her hands as though it was red hot. Wrapping her arms around her chest, she would have cried had she been able. Her lungs felt on fire, her heart punctured and bleeding. It pounded in her ears.

Outside the sounds of agitated mountain lions snarled and growled. Screeching roars echoed off of the sides of the valley, and then they added the scent of their own blood throughout the hollow.

~*~*~*~

Calla woke up in the house on the steps that led up to the attic. She wasn't dead, she wasn't outside, and her entrails weren't hanging out. She was naked, but that happened. Lifting her

4

head, she saw light from an overshadowed sun ebbed through the windows. She was disoriented. Ecstatic, yes. But she'd expected to wake up, if she woke up at all, outside. Had the *toms* gotten into the house? She started to sit up, but gasped at the pain that surged through her.

Running her tongue along her teeth, she tasted blood. She touched her mouth, her nose, but whatever blood was there had dried. She raised her head, more carefully this time. The ringing in her ears was receding. Her arm ached, but she could move it today. She couldn't pull in a deep breath, still, and she was pretty certain she couldn't put much weight on her leg, yet.

Thank you, Jesus!

Somehow, she had survived the night. The moon had let her heal up, maybe enough to survive tonight. She had no idea what time it was but if her momma had preached anything, it was modesty. Calla had an ingrained aversion to being naked in the daylight. With careful movements, she managed to make it to the bedroom by using the walls. She dressed and collapsed at the kitchen table with a bowl of puffed, tasteless cereal and not enough milk to cover the bottom of the bowl. It was 5:10 in the evening.

She ate regardless, hurriedly, and wolfed down another three pieces of bread, wishing she had time to toast them with butter—and put half a pig on them but there wasn't enough time. She needed to get the rifle and the knives and scoot up the stairs before moonrise. It came crazy early in the east in February. She gained a few extra minutes because of the ridgeline. But not many.

Buoyed by hope from making it through the first night, she dared to hope some more. Maybe God was still watching or listening. Maybe. Maybe the boys would get bored, or lost, or distracted and stay away tonight, too. Another night to heal and—

And then what?

Momma had always been there when she woke up. The boys were gone and Momma made her eggs and cheese and toast and sausage. What did she do when she Changed? Did she go out gallivanting and screaming at the moon, too? Did Momma lock her up in the cellar? Or the attic? She had asked her, just about every time. And Momma would tell her it was all right; she hadn't done anything horrible; she hadn't killed anything; and she was safe. Her cat didn't know how to get outside, right? If Calla locked the doors, locked herself in the attic and barred the door, and nothing got in— she couldn't get out either, right?

It was worth a try. She crawled and limped and crawled again to each of the windows and doors and made sure they were locked. The front yard was already dark in the shadow of the ridge. She kept the rifle with her, used it as a crutch, and hoped the boys stayed away. Maybe they were scared. Maybe last night had been real cats and her fear and hurt had made her think things were worse than they were. Maybe there weren't any boys coming around this time.

But a boy did come. She almost missed the movement when she glanced out the window except he turned to the side and there was a glint from his chest. Broad shoulders, strong arms, clearly glowing eyes, watching intensely, stalking something.

Her.

Calla's heart fell to her stomach as she dropped to a crouch that sent pain screaming through her leg. She bit back a whimper. It was Haben. It had to be. No one else could've blended into the shadows like that. No one else held himself like he did. No one else could cause both fear and hope in her chest at the same time. No one else made her stutter over her words and want to talk to him anyway.

"Haben?" she shouted.

He stopped and stared hard at the house, only his topaz eyes moving. He couldn't see her. Now that she knew where he was, and who he was, and with the moon trudging ever higher, she could see him plainly.

"What're you doing here?"

"I've not seen you in town this month," he called back. His accent was rich, from someplace south, he said; way, way south.

"I wanted to know why."

He'd been watching for her?

He moved his arms purposefully to his back and brought around a small, heart-shaped box with a stuffed, plush kitten attached. "I bring something."

With everything she was, she wanted to rush out and hold onto him and plead with him to stay and take care of everything, like Momma had done. She tightened her fingers around the gun stock.

She checked the tremor in her voice and said more strongly, "Now's a bad time!"

His head moved down and then up. "I know about you."

An icy cold hand wrapped around her chest. If he was a Shifter, she should've been able to sense it in him, as well. But she hadn't. And that'd be the only way he could distinguish. "What do you know?"

"I know about the moon. And how it sings. To its children. And what it brings to you."

Calla squinted. The moon was a harsh master and she a wretched slave-thing forced to become something not human; to behave like an animal. There was no singing, no beckoning lullaby. There was only screeching and crying and fighting for the control the moon twisted away from her.

It had been a year ago when Calla had met Haben at the dollar store on a day she and Momma had needed corn syrup and safety pins. She remembered she'd been staring at the stuffed animals and heart-shaped boxes that had chocolate in them.

At first glance, the boy called Haben had been like no one she'd ever seen before. Second glance, he was just so easy on the eyes she nearly sighed. Third glance he caught her watching him and smiled. She'd been lost.

Was Haben a Shifter? She supposed he could've found his way here by asking around town. But it was February. He worked in an apple orchard. She had presumed with winter he would return to his family in Costa Rica. It was where he sent all his money, he'd told her. Otherwise he would have had enough to buy her a small, red heart-shaped box with a plush kitten on top, he'd teased—right before Momma dragged her out of the store to the grocery.

"This," he said and she brought her attention back to where he stood in the deepening darkness of the yard. He moved a finger beneath the knotted hemp choker he wore at his neck. A symbol rested on his throat, made from wound grass, yarn and pewter. It was round, with three shapes that looked like raindrops, and three crossed lines through them. She remembered. He wore it all the time. "*Abuela*, my grandmother, she was *sacerdotisa*," he told her, his voice carrying on the night air. "She make this for me. So other *cambiadors* do not sense me."

"Cam-bee-what?"

He looked down for just a second, thinking. "Changers."

"Shifters?"

"*Sí!*" He nodded once. He still held the stuffed cat and the heart-shaped box out to his side. His eyes narrowed. "Can I come in?"

She wanted to trust him. But was it Haben she wanted to trust? Or was she scared, and isolated, and grieving, and wanted to trust anyone? Her mother had warned her. Almost daily. Can't trust the boys; can't trust the *toms*. They don't think right. The Change comes and they smell your sex and they show up from nowhere to take, and then they leave.

She squeezed the hilt of the rifle. "You need to go away," she shouted. "It's night and the moon is full."

It was too much of a coincidence that Haben would show up, the Crow Moon on the horizon, her in her Heat cycle of the Change. He must've sensed her, smelled her. The blood hadn't helped. She didn't want to hurt Haben. She realized that unexpectedly as her hand gripped the rifle stock. But she wasn't going to be owned, either. Her mother had been free of a leash. She would be, too.

Momma, a single mother who wouldn't have a job away from her daughter. She still had to provide food and shoes. She sold aprons and bag holders she sewed together when the season was warm, traveling to the town and the post office once a month for the help check. Protecting her from *boors*. There was only survival.

When she and Momma walked through town, people watched them. They stared. She wanted to know why. Was it her, she'd ask? Could they see what she was in the daylight?

"It's not anything to bother over, daughter-mine," Momma told her. "What they see when they look at you, is what they're fool-heads let them. A girl with wheat-colored hair and big green eyes that's prettier than they usually see. They don't see none of the Change. Maybe they can sense it, some of them. The girls don't like it. But the boys, they do. They want to own it. Don't be owned, girl. The boy you want is the one who sees beyond the pretty, below the shadow, into the heart of who you *are."*

But Momma had died. And Calla had forgotten most everything but her loss and fear and the moon and the Change.

"The smell of blood, it is everywhere, Calla." Haben had made no attempt to move away, much less leave. "Are you all right? Where is your *madre?*"

"She's here," she lied, suddenly feeling emboldened that he didn't know it was a lie. The mere presence of Momma had made many a *tom* spit, or cower and run off. "Now go on! Before you get hurt!"

"Others will come, Calla."

Her blood ran cold at his clear words, his change in stance and strategy.

"We can take care of ourselves," she said with more courage than she had left in her. If Momma were still here, she could have taken care of all of them.

"They kill your *madre*. They know you are alone."

"I'm not alone!" she screamed.

But she was. God in Heaven, she was utterly alone and while 'helpless' was never a word Momma would ever use, it was a heavy, crushing word right now, making her eyes blur with hot tears and her breath ache in her chest.

"Let me in." His words were quieter, but just as clear. Demanding. Persuading. "Let me help you."

Calla gritted her teeth and squeezed her eyes until her vision cleared. "Why? Why would I do that?"

"Because I can help," he told her simply. "Because I want to. Because you need help right now."

A whine caught in her throat. She didn't need help. She didn't need anyone. Momma had taught her everything she needed to know. How to hide. How to shoot to kill. How to bury a body.

She'd not seen a true Valentine card since eighth grade. That spring she'd had her first Change and she'd not been back to the school. That was five years ago now? Six? Things were different in the hollow. Time was different when it was kept from full moon to full moon and Heat to Heat.

She stopped at a rack in the dollar store when she saw the hearts, all red, shiny metallic. And the stuffed teddy bears. "What are these, Momma?" she had asked.

"These are for people with more money than sense. They buy 'em to show their beloved how much they are in love."

"I love you."

"There's no love like a mother and daughter's love, Calla."

She was staring at a stuffed cat when someone picked it up and handed it to her. She looked up into the coffee eyes of a boy's dark face. Darker than just being out in the sun could make it. He wasn't like the others. He wasn't mountain lion caramel, he was much darker, like a jungle cat. Dark molasses skin. He was tall, maybe older than her, maybe just looked older. When he smiled, he had white, white teeth. "You like this?"

She could only lift her shoulder and look away and marvel at how her heart pounded when there was no moon out at all over High Lonesome, West Virginia. He'd followed them over to the grocery store; coming upon them again at the potatoes or in the spaghetti aisle. Always with that smile, his teeth flashing so white and the hint of a dimple at the corner of his mouth.

She watched his head swivel to the right. One hand still out to his side, the other holding the kitten candy box. "They are coming, Calla. Let me in."

Did he hear them? Did she? *Boors* usually didn't travel in clusters. Only rarely, like during Heat. Few girls, too many boys. The blood pounded in her ears, making it hard to think. The moon was coming up. She felt lightheaded, from fear, from euphoria, from the constant prickliness of her own skin she couldn't ignore any longer. She did need help. And dear Lord, if she had to die tonight, it might as well be him.

"Haben!" she shouted. "Come in here, then!"

~*~*~*~

To the best of Calla's knowledge, there'd never been a man in the house. There'd never been anybody in the house that she knew of, except for herself and Momma. Having Haben in the same room with her alone seemed all sorts of wrong. It made her feel faint. Made her forget about the stabbing in her chest. And made her hurt all the worse when she tried to breathe normally.

Haben had taken one look at her and cussed. She assumed. It wasn't her language, but the delivery was the same. He set about getting water and bandages and ordered her to lie down while he tried to clean her off and fix her up. She wouldn't lie down. She told him she had no idea if she'd be able to get back up or not. That was true. But she wouldn't put herself in that position of submission with a *tom* here so close and her in her Heat cycle. That was just asking for trouble.

He kept his attention on her injuries, on wrapping them securely, on looking for her a crutch or a cane to help get up the stairs. She focused on his eyes and his lips. His eyes were the most beautiful she'd ever seen. They'd been dark brown in the store. Here they were the color of creamy caramel and it made her heart beat in her ears every time they met her gaze. His lips were dark and shaped with a stern current underneath, which looked positively suckable when he bit the bottom one in concentration. She wondered if maybe God had made them so dark so his teeth would shine all the more white when they flashed a quick smile. She bet his teeth were long and sharp when he shifted.

"You are a Shifter, right?"

He glanced at her. She wished he would just let her stare at his eyes. "*Sí*, yeah."

"A cat—? Uh, that is, what kind?"

He smirked a little. The corner of his mouth made a black crease she wanted to touch. "A cat," he affirmed. "*Un leopardo.*"

"Leopard?" she repeated to make sure it was the same.

He nodded.

"Me, too," she said, instantly feeling a blush of embarrassment. He knew that already. Besides, Momma had said to never talk about it. Never. She swallowed, looking down to where he was wrapping her arm and elbow with a towel he'd ripped since they'd run out of bandages with her leg. "I mean, you know, a cat. Mountain lion."

"*Sí, puma.* All I've found here are mountain lion." He glanced up at her. "All males. No females."

"Yeah," she breathed out. "I reckon there's not a lot. The way they come around here. The *boors.*"

"Boors?"

"The *toms*," she nodded. "The males."

"Ah." He made a knot at her elbow and tightened it. "How does that feel?"

"It hurts," she said, still watching his face.

"Cracked ribs, ankle, or leg maybe. I don't know about the arm. Your Change should fix things better. What happen?"

"I fell." It sounded as stupid when she said it aloud as it did when she heard it in her head. She swung herself off of the cabinet, grimacing when she put her weight on her legs. He handed her the cane. "You shouldn't be here." It was far too late to put forth that argument and there was no force behind it.

"I am here already. What happened to your mother?"

She squinted at him. "You acted like you knew already."

"It was a guess. *Machos* in town … *más* brazen lately." He did not elaborate.

She stared down at the floor swallowing hard. "Last month, the Wolf Moon." She glanced up. "There were three or four *toms* came out. It was raining ice that night, too. Two got her. She died from fever."

Her sight blurred and she wiped at her eyes more embarrassed than before. But Haben simply nodded. "I'm sorry. I'm sorry I wasn't here."

Calla shook her head. "You didn't know. Plus it's not your place."

Haben put his hand on her shoulder. "I knew you two were without *campeón*. Your mother should not have to defend your honor alone all these years."

"My h-honor?" Calla frowned. She wouldn't have put it that way. Momma had always been there, protecting her, teaching her. But honor? "We had each other. We didn't need any other companions."

The smile was faint. "*Campeón* is a guardian. The *cambiadors,* the Shifters in my home, the principal male watch over his territory, to protect the females. If there is no male to oversee, someone will step up to the job."

"We did all right." She said it resentfully, but as soon as she heard the words in her own ears, the ache of grief hit her. *All right up until they killed her.*

"How did you guess? How'd you know she was dead? That someone had killed her?"

He exhaled. "I didn't. The," he searched for the right word, "scent in town, it was different. It was sharper, thinner. The difference between the orange to the *limón.* The males, they were smug, talking louder. I taste the confidence. I only guessed outside, when it struck me that the taste was *soberbia.*" He looked at her and interpreted, "Pride."

"So," her eyes fell, "they know."

"They think they know. They at least know that maybe the momma cat won't be up to measure."

Calla closed her eyes tight.

Haben spoke through her misery. "She taught you well. You survive untouched this whole time. But now," he glanced at the window, "let someone else help, yes? You gonna need it."

She half-laughed, half-sobbed and wiped at her face again. "Yeah, I think you may be right. But–"

"But?"

"But what about you? It's my Heat Change."

His face went as still as his breath. She felt as though she'd said something terribly wrong; wrong enough that he might leave and she didn't know how to make him stay. He shouldn't be here. She was right about that, she knew she was. But now that he was here, she didn't want him to leave.

"Yeah." His voice was so heavy when he exhaled the words it made her heart ache. He looked down and then back into her gaze. "I don't know. I will not Change all the way. Maybe it will help."

"What?"

He looked at her intently. She felt like he was trying to read her mind, to know everything she and Momma had gone through the last six years. "Your mother. She was Shifter?"

"I – I think so. I never saw it, though."

He thought a moment more before he nodded. "Could be. After the female mates, she resist; better to protect the kit. But ... you a little old for a kit, are you not?"

She wondered if he was poking fun, but she saw the crease at the side of his mouth again and knew she was being teased. "It was just me and Momma," she defended. "I thought I was ready. But maybe—maybe there's more I don't know."

"Your mother, she did teach you this control?"

"Control?" She frowned. What was that he had said? "You can *not* Change all the way?"

He nodded. "The more it stops, the better memory. And if you can remember, you can think beyond the moment."

"That's what I need," she said breathlessly. "Teach me how."

"It took me four tries. My brother, it took nine." He grinned sadly. "We have just ... a little time? I don't think I can teach you so quickly."

"Try," she urged. "You have to try. I learn quick. I've had to learn everything quick. I will do it, I promise. I just don't want–I don't want them–"

He gripped her hand. "I don't know that I can teach you," he told her firmly. "We may have to fight, again."

"I'm tired of fighting." She grasped the words at the same time she said them. And she realized with a twist in her gut that it was the absolute truth. Momma had never said there would be a time when she wouldn't be fighting. Maybe she thought that's all there would be, fighting, month after month, hiding, and the life or death struggle during Heat. But God in Heaven, losing Momma was hard. And it made the desire to fight hard. She didn't want to fight anymore.

"I just… want to live like everyone else does. Not like this. Not hidden away. Not scared. Not knowing what to do on a – on a Saturday—or a Tuesday night—or wonder why Taco Bell is so great—or what Instagram is—and have a cell phone. All I *know* is that I will have to fight when the moon is full. Nobody else does that. I don't want to, either."

Haben hesitated and inhaled deeply. "I know." He offered her a nod. "We … will try. But do not think it failure if you can't tonight. We will fight so you try another night."

She swallowed. "Momma wanted me to be free. No leash. To make my own way. My own choices." She searched his face. "But they were her choices. Weren't they?"

"She did good, teaching you. She was just taken too soon, I think."

"I need to learn this." She seized his fingers. "I can be free then. With that control I can be free."

"Maybe." He did not look very confident at the prospect.

~*~*~*~

They had moved to the loveseat in the den. She was nervous, excited, anxious, prickly and very nearly hummed with anticipation.

"You have to decide to Change."

She blinked, expecting more. That was his big revelation, his great secret?

"I don't get to *decide*," she insisted. "It just happens."

"And you don't want it to," Haben said.

She clenched her hands. "Of course I don't want it to."

"That is the first problem."

Anyone else and she might have felt as though her intelligence had been insulted, but his eyes were so kind, so easy to feel comfortable in, that she merely waited for him to explain.

"You fight it. You fight who you are. You are gifted, Calla. You have…abilities. It is power. It is life. It is life before there were towns or cities. You are a survivor of a race that was bred to survive. You cannot hold control and to be fighting in the same time. You have to embrace and then control."

She slumped into the cushion. "I don't know anything but fighting. And apparently I don't do it very well." The clock on the wall ticked loudly.

He offered a small smile she found encouraging. "It is easier to stop fighting than you think. Close your eyes." She did. Her heart skipped a beat when he put his hand over hers. "What are you, Calla?"

What was she? A girl. A daughter. An orphan. Alone. No, what was she? When she lay in bed at night and heard the stars and smelled the frogs and felt the subtle seasonal shifts and saw herself in her mind's eye; what did she see?

"I'm a Shifter." She whispered it, but it felt like rolling thunder along her soul when she heard it glide from her tongue.

"*Sí.* You are one who changes."

"I can change," she murmured, awed at the sudden impact that knowledge held. She swallowed. It tasted salty.

"And you are more than that. You are Calla, from a great line of animal shifters that go back to when the moon was first formed. They are proud and you have the same right. They have passed that along to you. Calla? Do you hear me?"

She felt his hand on her shoulder, and then felt his fingers in her hair. She nodded and the feel of his fingertips brushing her neck made goose bumps down her back. "Who are you?"

"I'm Calla," her voice was husky. "I can change. I'm a Shifter."

"True. But you are more. You are Calla of the Mountain Lion race. *Reina.* You are the only Queen from mountain top to mountain top."

The word *queen* was discordant. It made her feel strange and conspicuous. She was anything but regal.

"Do you not know? This *is your* territory, Calla. It is not theirs. This is your home. Yours. They are base and listen to nothing but hunger. You hear more. You know more. You want more."

The term took on a greater meaning beneath his guidance. He was not placing a pedestal beneath her. There were not powerful monarchial stepmothers or fairy tale princesses. No poisonous apples or glass slippers. This was primal.

His words moved down her insides until she felt a deep, liquid warmth growing. A rhythmic pulsing at her core she no longer wanted to ignore. "I do want more."

"You need to accept. Who you are, what you are, what you can be. To harness it."

Harness. Her breath hitched. "No leash."

There was silence. Long and longing. God, had she broken something? Haben's commitment? Her momma's heart? She wanted to cry.

"Yes, Calla."

Air rushed from her lungs in relief. She listened to his voice again, coveting it as though it was water in the middle of a drought.

"A lead; a leash. Your leash. Your own. Not someone else's. Only Calla should hold the great cat's leash. Only you have that right."

Her eyes were still closed and her breathing was faster. Haben smelled so right, there in front of her, and his voice was sweet warm maple syrup over her senses. She wanted a taste of him and had no idea how to ask.

"You are so very strong. I hear it now. You have hidden it away. It is your decision and yours alone, Calla. Your choices. Your future."

"How?" she whispered.

"Not how," he corrected. "When. You decide, not them. Allowing them to decide, gives them the leash."

"No," her voice broke, "leash."

She vibrated all over. The moon was above the ridgeline and it called to her so she could not ignore it. Not a cry, not a lullaby. But was it a song? Was Haben right about that? She had always heard the cries of a captive. The sound of a whip, a decree that she was powerless to avoid, commands that went against her own desires. Powerful drumming in her chest that made her cower in fear.

But it was not a march to war. Not to her death or to bring death. When she opened her ears, it was a sound that awakened; one composed to not keep the cat's eyes closed any longer. It was a reveille. It wasn't meant to be resisted. It was meant to be embraced so that the moon, her history, could bestow upon her the strength and power she was designed to contain. And command. It was a rallying cry. It wasn't hiding in shadows, it wasn't death. It was life and power and control. Her gift. She just had to take it.

"When." She was panting. "Haben." She opened her eyes. He was crouched in front of her, beautiful dark brown-sugar fur covering him, embellished with black rings. His eyes were smoky crystal staring at her from a wide, feline visage.

The Change came. He moved back when she fell whimpering to all fours. It was terrible. The pain coursed through her chest like a crushing flood of fire causing white hot lightning in her skull. Her face twisted in agony where she writhed on the floor. Only the years of conditioning kept her from shrieking from the onslaught. Fur crept up her bowed back and sprouted down her arms. Finger bones cracked and shrank. Talons split the skin on her fingertips and burst through.

"Calla! Stop!"

Her eyes opened, already able to see ultraviolet temperatures and shimmery magnetic currents. It was disorienting, alien and surreal.

"Hooow?" she wailed.

"No. *When*," he rasped. "When. You must know the cat and tame her."

Tame her?

She let out a miserable whine. Her long, tan tail glided from the base of her spine. The breath left her lungs as her legs bent back on themselves. The moan was long and low from her chest when her joints elongated for added leverage.

Momma had wanted to protect her. A single mother was difficult enough; protecting her from *boors* once a month, exhausting. There was only survival. Only training to hide and to fight. But to tame it? Control it? Momma hadn't known how. She would have said.

Don't be owned, girl.

The voices mixed in her head.

You want more.

She didn't want to fight any longer. She'd thought she didn't have any fight left in her since Momma's death. But she found that wasn't true. She did want more. She was the only one who could find it. She was the only one who could stop it.

I AM more.

Her eyes opened. They were feline and glowed pale green. Behind them was Calla. And she stared at Haben.

She removed the tattered clothes.

"All right," she growled. "Let's take care of this."

~*~*~*~

Weapons ready, they went to the porch. Knives in sheaths at waist and thighs, and Calla with the rifle from Momma's bedroom. The moon was barely above the ridge. Distinctly antagonistic yowls could be heard through the hollow. Those vying for the right to take her first. She glanced over at Haben. He offered her an encouraging nod, his black mouth parting a feline smile. She shouldn't feel like smiling. She was just coming into her own, controlling the cat in a form the cat was unfamiliar with, and faced the fight of her life. And yet, she couldn't help but feel her heart lift at the confidence he showed in her.

While the posturing continued in long, low wails on the summit, a mountain lion braved the forefront and came at them from the darkness. Calla's pupils dilated. She held the rifle steady, staring at her mark, but Haben moved in front of her and met the interloper in the yard. Calla squinted. All she had wanted was for somebody to come and protect her like Momma had done all those years. Now that Haben was here, she wanted nothing more than the opportunity to show them all how she could play king of the hill with the boys. Or queen of the hollow, as the case may be.

The cat's ears were back. It hissed, its mouth curled open showing most of its teeth. In his 'hybrid' state, Haben was more than twice the cat's size. He stared hard at its glinting obsidian eyes, but the cat didn't leave. It hunkered down and whined at Haben. But didn't turn tail and run. The yowling seemed closer. Apparently it did to Haben, too. He wasted no more time in intimidating the challenger and stopped it with a swipe on its face. It sprang backward, blood seeping to the surface from two long slash marks. It made a half-hearted attempt to save its dignity with a piercing squall. Haben advanced a single step and it skittered off into the brush.

Haben had no chance to reach the stairs before two more cats raced for the house. One leapt over the rail without pausing. Calla put a leg back to brace herself, the stronger one without the makeshift splint. She met her assailant with a knee to its stomach. She felt its harsh breath against her face. In the next heartbeat, she brought her knife across its chest, just missing its throat. But close enough. She grinned to see the surprise and fear in the *boor's* eyes. She watched it scamper into the night. Yeah, she wanted more of that.

The other had lunged at Haben, clawing and biting and tearing at the flesh of his exposed chest. He caught the cat around the neck. He jerked it to the ground hard enough to stun it. But not before it had managed to rake massive rear claws over Haben's belly. Calla called out his name when she saw him stagger. Quick enough he regained his equilibrium. He opened his mouth and roared, sending the fur down Calla's spine standing on end. It had a similar effect on the cougar. The cat spat twice as it bounded back and finally ran out of sight.

The scent of Haben's blood mix assailed Calla's senses of smell and taste and brought heat blooming through her. She licked her lips. She had to concentrate. There was more than enough newness to absorb tonight without lust interfering. She picked up the sound of padded feet racing from the woods to their right. It had to have smelled the blood, too. The cougar raced in with single-minded speed. It threw itself on top of Haben, tearing out a hunk of flesh from his shoulder. Another darted from the side. It aimed for his wounded belly.

Calla hissed. *Toms* never traveled in packs. That was for the base, the wolves and the coyotes. Where the hell were they all coming from? She licked the sensitive buds beneath her nose, tasting Haben's scent and she realized what was happening all at once.

We may have to fight, again, he had told her.

Haben had been here the night before. It had been his growls she'd heard so close to the door. It had been him fighting, standing in the gap between her door and the heat-crazed *boors*. Until he could come and see about her for himself. They had been routed, but only to regroup. To get others. As many as they could find. And they returned in force tonight. They just weren't going to take her. They intended to get rid of Haben, too.

"Oh, hell, no," she rumbled, re-cocking the gun. Calla preferred the rifle with the hope of getting in clean shots and not risking Haben.

Haben grabbed the muzzle of the first puma, gory with his own meat and blood, and flung the cat onto the approaching male. It only slowed it a little, but enough that Haben managed to rip his claws across the cat's face. Its scream of rage was cut off by another slash across its throat. To that it began dragging itself off.

The other was up and arched to pounce.

Calla leveled the shotgun and fired. With a feral cry, it was thrown back and it too scuttled away. The echo ricocheted gratifyingly through the hollow.

The first cougar had stopped moving at the edge of the yard and lay still. But another mountain lion bounded over the body, and one came from behind Calla's peripheral. It knocked her down before she could bring around the rifle barrel. When Haben whirled to go to her, he was struck down, too. Sharp, deadly teeth buried in his shoulder. Another inch and it would have been his neck.

The cat held Calla down, claws in her shoulders, saliva falling on her face. It stared into her gaze, its dark red eyes smoldering. There was fury there, and there was lust. It yowled his dominance as much as its victory.

Her rifle was out of reach. Calla hissed back at him. She wasn't going to be taken so easily. Besides, Haben needed her help right now. She strained upward and managed to bite down hard on its chin. She twisted her head, grating off chunks of flesh. It shrieked in shock and pain, momentarily recoiling. She pulled up both legs before it could lunge again and kicked it backwards.

She was on the balls of her feet when it regained his. Not eager for a repeat, it circled her, whining a warning. Calla drew a knife from the wrap on her thigh, tossed it up, and caught it with her other hand.

"You best run." She showed her long teeth, shining in the moonlight.

The cat sputtered a series of spits she was sure were cussings.

"I said run," she ordered with a hiss and threw her knife. It embedded with a satisfying thud in the shoulder. The cougar cringed, shrieked, and tried without success to reach the knife with its teeth. Its large feline head swung around looking for escape.

"Wait!" Calla ordered. To her surprise, the cat obeyed. She flashed a toothy grin. "That's my knife." Before it could react, she sprang forward, twisted the blade as she pulled it free and was back into a ready stance while the cat wailed. It snarled at her a last time, then leapt over the porch railing and disappeared.

Haben stood up from the ground and shook his head. Calla snatched up the gun and took one step from the wooden deck to help him. Haben held out one hand. "No. Back," he rasped. This cat was bigger than the others. If cougars formed prides, and this pride had an alpha, this one would have been it.

"Mine."

He crouched and shifted to all fours into full leopard, muscular, taut, dark, and a full hand-span bigger than the intruder. He growled. Calla's stomach fell. Suddenly, this was more than a fight for home and virtue. Her lips curled back and she tasted the air. This was a fight for dominance and the *toms,* including Haben, were dangerously close to a blood-fury.

The other stalked forward. Haben emitted one final, threatening keen of warning for the cougar to leave peacefully. The cat replied with a snarl. He advanced. They circled one another until Haben feinted forward. The cat flinched. Then charged. Haben dragged his claws across the cat's gut. It tumbled backward, hit the ground, and came to its feet howling. It kept the rip in its flank faced away as it paced, its unblinking eyes fixed on Haben.

There were only three heartbeats between attacks. The cougar launched itself fast and low, knocking the legs out from under the leopard. Haben rolled, his jaws reaching for the cat, but it twisted and slammed him down on the hard ground. He grunted, the air driven from his lungs. But almost as soon as he hit, he swiveled, snapping at the cat and catching part of the flesh at its ribs. They separated and in less time than it took to draw a breath, they crashed together again, Haben digging his claws into the cat's back, and the cat raking at the leopard's vulnerable belly. With a desperate need to protect himself, Haben dislodged them from one another. The cat pressed its advantage, on him immediately, driving him back toward the house, toward Calla. Claws whipped across Haben's face, knocking him back so that he stumbled. The cougar tore at his body, managing to bite hard into his thigh, nearly going to bone, refusing to let go, pulling at the flesh and sinew, determined to get to the artery. He rolled forward, driving the cat to its back, its fangs still holding bits of Haben's leg clinging to them. They rolled on the ground, each trying to gain their feet while guarding their weaknesses.

They were slick with blood when both spun away. With another hiss, they pivoted to stalk and circle. The cougar's rear foot slid on the blackened grass. Barely noticeable, but enough. Haben reversed his direction and sprung. The other tried to leap away, but had lost valuable traction. Haben slammed his head into its throat. The cat choked and Haben was on top of him, sinking his huge teeth into the neck of the mountain lion.

He stayed atop it, refusing to let go despite the futile raking it did to the leopard's underbelly. Despite the pitiful whines that came after. Finally it lay still, bleeding, but breathing.

~*~*~*~

Haben unlocked his jaw. He turned to Calla. She dared to stare at him levelly and swallowed. He had secured the right to take her. She knew that much instinctively.

She moved into a defensive stance. She didn't know how much good it would do. Haben had bested at least six attackers. She didn't stand a chance if he decided to take her during the full moon Heat. Her rapid breaths came out in small puffs in the February air where she stared at him from the top step. His lips curled back from his teeth and she heard him hiss. It was gentle, but firm. They both knew what he had won.

She backed up one pace. "Haben," she said, surprised her voice didn't wobble, "this is my home."

He advanced a step and she retreated one.

"Mine," she repeated.

He hissed and she could almost make out the word in the sound.

Momma had wanted her to be able to make her own decisions.

"This is my birthright, now, Haben," she said with more confidence. "You wanted me to accept it. Right? Well, now I have."

He stalked toward her another step.

"You can't take from me."

He took another step toward her and she stood her ground.

"Haben." She wouldn't beg. It wasn't in her. "Haben." He took another step and his maw opened, simultaneously smelling and tasting her in Heat. He licked his lips. When she looked down at him, she noticed for the first time the necklace he had been wearing. It lay on her chest now. Somehow he had managed to put it on her. When he was schooling her? Helping her? When she had changed?

"Haben, my beautiful leopard. You can't take what I'd give you freely."

He stopped. His bright, topaz eyes gazed into her glowing green ones. She lifted the handmade amulet with a partially furred, clawed finger, looking at it first and then showing him. He hesitated. A spark of something other than lust glinted in his face.

"Let me let you know my heart."

It felt like the moon stood still. Then without so much as a sigh, he collapsed as Haben the man on the stairs of her house. She knelt immediately and lifted his head. He was conscious, but injured and bleeding in a dozen places or more, some—like his side and leg— very badly. She pulled him inside the house, onto the couch, and barred the doors. While washing her hands off, she realized she had reverted, also. To Calla, naked but no longer so afraid. She wondered how that had occurred. Haben would tell her. She should be able to control that, too. Evidently he could. She washed off quickly, pulled on a robe, and gathered alcohol, sulfur and what torn towels were left to bandage up the wounds. This she knew. This she took from Momma.

"Le pido perdón, Calla," he said, his voice just a whisper. She threw an afghan over his hips. He reached up and rubbed his thumb along her cheek.

She merely shook her head, wiping blood from his jaw and nose.

"I am…so sorry, Calla," he repeated. "It is your decision."

She looked at him and this time smiled. "I know." She leaned in and kissed him on the lips gently, like they did on television. It was a lot warmer, and a lot tenser, and a lot more pleasant than she had thought it'd be. "Thank you."

He relaxed a little.

She returned back to work on the gashes and rakes. The wound in his side was clotting already, but it was deep. It was far too soon to have to be doing this again. She'd lost Momma. There was a knot in her stomach too large to try to hide. "You're going to have to Change," she said huskily. "You're going to have to and let your leopard heal you up."

"I will."

"I mean it, Haben." She looked into his caramel eyes. "I won't stand for anybody dying in my hollow any more, what they don't come asking for it."

"I will," he insisted gently. "I will." His wounds obviously hurt but he breathed shallowly through them and did not let them stop him. "I wanted to ask something. But it … it is nice to hear you say it."

She frowned down at him. "I ain't saying it because it sounds good. I'm saying it because I don't want any more death in my house."

He smirked. "Oh, I believe you, *reina.* That is not what I mean. I mean to hear you say it is yours; this is yours."

She glanced down, cleaning more blood from his chest and arm, considering his words. She nodded. "It is mine," she said quietly. "I'll claim it. I don't want to lose it." She met his gaze again. "I don't want to lose you either."

"I am not dying here. I've had worse."

She couldn't resist a lopsided grin. "You're such a liar."

He merely shrugged, but then grimaced at the pain.

"Shush, now. I'm busy. Let me get you wrapped up to stop what bleeding I can. I got something for pain, too. Then you'll have to change. The sun'll be up before we know it."

"A new day." He smiled.

His smile took away her reasoning and made her respond in kind without realizing it. "Somethin' like that." She shook her head at herself and gave him a stern quirk of her mouth.

"There is more to see to. Who are these men that they come with ferocity?"

She lifted a shoulder. "It's always been that way."

"I will Change. By tomorrow night I should be much better again, *si.*"

"You'd better be," she said with false gravity.

He exhaled and shook his head.

"What?"

"This ... isn't how I wanted Valentine's Day. I thought about it—about you—all year long. How I was going to bring chocolate and talk to your *madre.*"

She looked down and swallowed.

"I'm sorry."

"No." She shook her head. "It's all right." She managed a grin. "I still have the chocolate. And a kitty."

He couldn't help but give a little smirk of his own. Her heart did a funny flip-flop at seeing it.

"Calla," he said, watching her eyes carefully, "would you ... go out with me? Sometime?"

She chuckled and put a lock of straw-colored hair behind her ear. "Would it mean being able to kiss you some more?"

"I think it might." The glint in his eye was irresistible.

"Then yeah," she said, nestling in closer. "I think I would."

He tilted his chin up as much as he could without it hurting, but she kept just out of his reach. He gave a little growl in his throat and raised his hand to cup the back of her head. She grinned and relented, kissing him, and letting him suckle her lips until he sighed and relaxed, and she sighed in contentment.

"I should Change now." He looked at the ceiling as if he were debating with the stars about it.

"You should."

He looked at her and she could tell he was tired and hurting. "You will stay, *si*? You'll be here when I wake?"

"Oh, yes," she assured him. "I'm not going anywhere. I'll watch over you, and I'll rub my hands on your fur, and later on I'll make breakfast with eggs and cheese, toast and sausage."

His eyes closed.

"And maybe after the moon beds down, I'll sing you something at sunrise."

"*Perfecto*," he mumbled. He changed into the leopard while she watched. In another heartbeat he exhaled with an exhausted groan. She situated herself beside him on the couch.

"Maybe not perfect," she said softly, running her fingers through the thick, soft fur on his head and beneath his ears. "But I think I've found the right lead to get there."

THE END

HEAVY HANDED

Jake Merritt is through with women, Kentucky, and the world in general. Eighty acres in the middle of nowhere should give Jake exactly what he wants after his ugly break-up: Solitude. Except the lady who only rises with the fog won't just up and leave when Jake orders her to do so.

Alicia is bound to Jake's land in ways she's not even sure about, and can't pick up and leave just because Jake's the new owner. There are crimes and curses to be exposed, uncovered, and broken.

Once Jake decides to believe Alicia's story, things take an ominous turn. Can Jake break the curse that holds Alicia and free himself to risk loving again?

ABOUT THE AUTHOR

Jacci DeVera lives in the southern Appalachians, and enjoys writing as much as she enjoys napping, cats, cookies, myths, and wolves. The only "rule" she has when she writes is that the story must have a happy ending. Romance was the natural choice to settle in.

She is thrilled with the direction writing, and particularly romance, has taken in recent years with genre lines blurring, so her love of fantasy, paranormal, and historicals can intermingle without concern for intolerance.

Jacci believes in the importance of the journey as much as the destination itself. Stories are found everywhere if we pause long enough to listen.

DARK HOLLOWS PRESS

Dark Hollows Press publishes all genres of romantic expression.

We believe our authors are artists and their talent shouldn't be censored, so our authors present high quality stories full of romance, desire, and sometimes graphic moments that are both entertaining and erotic. We have an exclusive group of talented writers and we publish stories that range from historical to fantasy, sci-fi to contemporary.

We invite you to visit us at www.darkhollowspress.com.

Dark Hollows Press